LATE ONE NIGHT, SAM THE LIBRARY MOUSE was hard at work. His friend Sarah dropped in and asked, "What are you doing, Sam? Writing a new book?"

Sam said, "I'm just making some notes and sketches in my journal. Maybe you'd like to try. I think I have an extra one you could use."

"No thanks," Sarah said, looking around. "You know, Sam, there's a place next door that has the kind of stuff you're looking at in these books. I think they call it a . . . a museum. We should go!"

"What?" Sam cried. "There's a museum, right next door?"

"Sure," Sarah said. "Come on, let's take a look! This is our chance to have some fun!"

Sam was nervous. He had never been outside the library before.

He thought and thought about what to do. Finally, he said, "Well, all right, I'll go. I'll take my journal along. But I want you to take one, too!"

"A journal?" Sarah exclaimed. "An explorer can't explore if she's writing in a journal. An explorer wants an adventure!"

"Then make an 'explorer's journal,'" replied Sam. "You can take a journal anywhere and put anything you want in it—pictures or souvenirs of your trip.

"You can use it to write down your thoughts and feelings about the things you see or the adventures you have. A museum would be a great place to take a journal!"

"Okay," Sarah said with a sigh, "I'll take one. But let's get moving! I'm ready for some adventure."

"Right now? But—"

"Come on!" Sarah said. "Explorers move fast!"

Sam hurried to fill his backpack with supplies and an extra journal for Sarah. Then the two friends crept beneath the library door and raced across the field beyond to the big building on the hill.

Once inside the museum, Sarah quickly found a pretty stamp and a checkroom ticket. "Can I put these in my journal?" she asked.

"Of course you can," Sam said, feeling very small among the giant and mysterious shadows. Then he glanced up. He let out a squeak when he saw a huge figure looming over him!

"Don't worry, Sam. It isn't real," Sarah said.

Sam breathed a sigh of relief. "You're right! The sign here says he's from ancient Greece!"

"But he's broken," said Sarah. "What happened to his spear and shield? And his nose?"

"He's very old," Sam said.

"I have an idea," Sarah said, getting out her journal.

"If I draw a picture of the sculpture, I can make him good as new . . . better, even, with some ears and a tail!"

"That's funny," Sam giggled. "Say, what's that over there?"

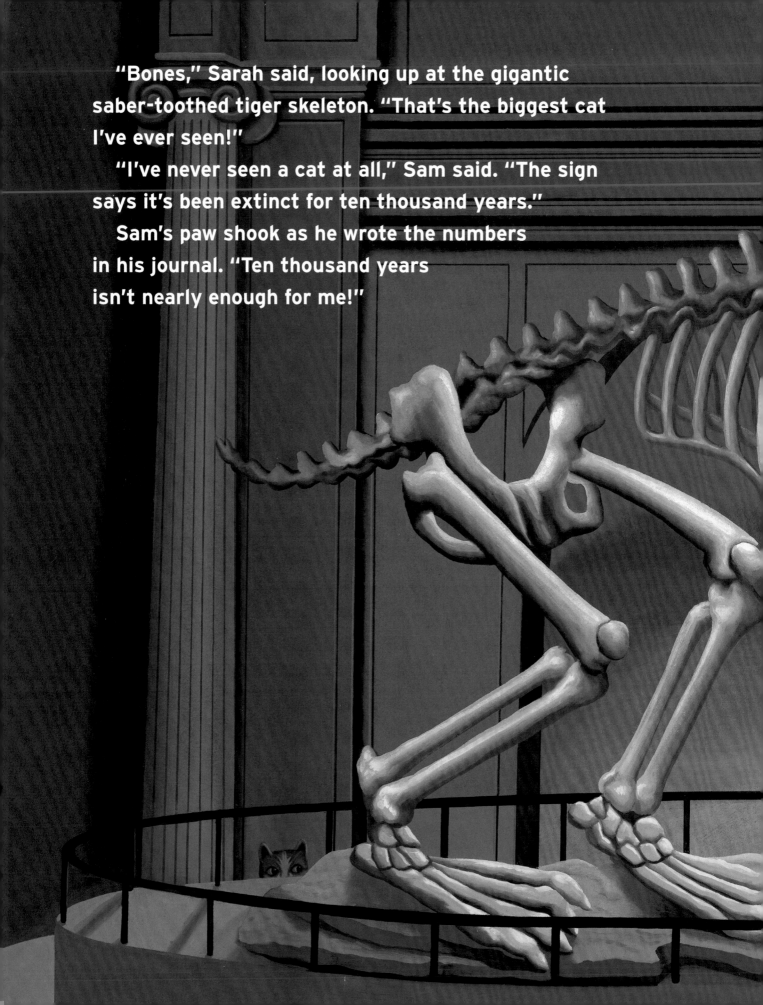

"Bones," Sarah said, looking up at the gigantic saber-toothed tiger skeleton. "That's the biggest cat I've ever seen!"

"I've never seen a cat at all," Sam said. "The sign says it's been extinct for ten thousand years."

Sam's paw shook as he wrote the numbers in his journal. "Ten thousand years isn't nearly enough for me!"

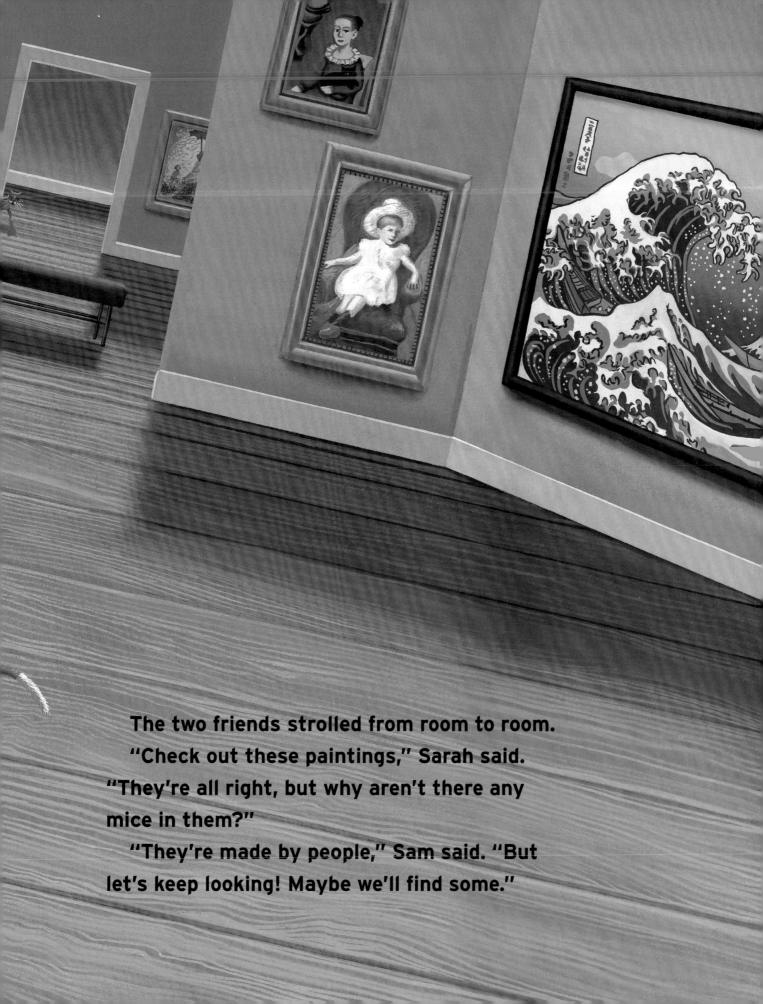

The two friends strolled from room to room.

"Check out these paintings," Sarah said.
"They're all right, but why aren't there any
mice in them?"

"They're made by people," Sam said. "But
let's keep looking! Maybe we'll find some."

Sam and Sarah looked at antique musical instruments,
old weapons, and suits of armor.

Sarah said, "Sam, I'm going to climb up to the top of that
rider's helmet, to see what the world looks like from up
there! I'll make a sketch in my journal, too. Want to come?"

"No," Sam said. "You're not supposed to touch
anything, Sarah. And museums aren't for climbing!"

The world looked awfully big to Sarah from the top of the suit of armor. But glancing down, she saw a dark figure creeping toward her friend. "Sam!" she cried. "Look out!"

Sarah leapt into the air and landed with a
WHOOMP on a cat's head!

The two mice scurried away as quickly as their
legs could carry them. "Faster, Sam," Sarah
squeaked. "Faster!"

They rounded a corner, found a darkened
stairwell, and scampered down the stairs.

A mole stood quietly along a wall. "Welcome
to the special galleries," he said. "Won't you
step inside?"

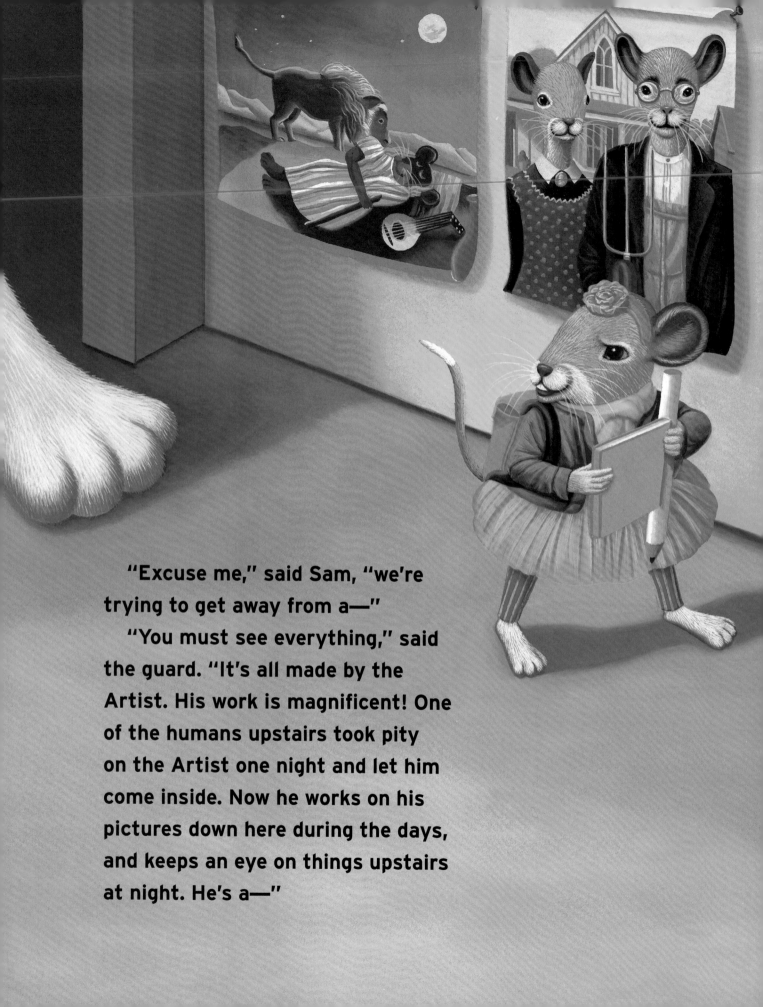

"Excuse me," said Sam, "we're trying to get away from a—"

"You must see everything," said the guard. "It's all made by the Artist. His work is magnificent! One of the humans upstairs took pity on the Artist one night and let him come inside. Now he works on his pictures down here during the days, and keeps an eye on things upstairs at night. He's a—"

"Cat!" Sarah cried.
She and Sam lifted their pencils like spears, and
held their journals like shields.

"Hold that pose!" the cat said. "It's absolutely *purrr*-fect."

Quick as a wink, the cat began to sketch. "I love mice," he said, "but I so seldom get to draw from life. I'm glad you decided to stop running away! I knew you two would make fabulous models."

"Meet the Artist," said the guard.

"A cat?" asked Sam, trembling.

"There's no need to be afraid," the mole said. "And wait until you see how he's drawn you! It will be good enough to frame and hang on the wall!"

"I have an idea," said Sarah. "Maybe when you're finished drawing us, Mr. Artist, I can draw a picture of you in my journal!"

"Fellow artists?" asked the cat.

"My friend Sam makes books," Sarah said.

"And my friend Sarah," said Sam, "keeps a pretty nice journal!"

When Sarah was finished with her sketch, the guard said, "Wonderful! It would look perfect hanging right by the entrance to the gallery. You wouldn't want to donate it, would you?"

Sarah looked at Sam.

"There are a lot of pages in that journal," Sam said. "I don't think it would hurt to spare just one!"

"As long as I have room for the Artist's autograph," Sarah said. "I'm not going home without it!"

When Sarah was finished with her sketch, the guard said, "Wonderful! It would look perfect hanging right by the entrance to the gallery. You wouldn't want to donate it, would you?"

Sarah looked at Sam.

"There are a lot of pages in that journal," Sam said. "I don't think it would hurt to spare just one!"

"As long as I have room for the Artist's autograph," Sarah said. "I'm not going home without it!"

"I guess an explorer *can* explore while writing and drawing in a journal," Sarah said, after they had said good-bye to their new friends.

"True," said Sam, "but an adventure is fun, too. It gives you something to write about!"

"Where shall we go next?" Sarah asked, as the sun came up behind the museum.

"I'm sure you'll dream up something," Sam said with a yawn, and the two mice headed back home to the library.

For Ivy

Author's Note

As soon as I was old enough to pick up a pencil, I knew that I was an artist. I learned to express my feelings and thoughts about the world through pictures. I also learned at an early age that we could see the work of famous artists as well as the artifacts of ancient cultures and faraway places in museums. So as often as I could, I visited museums to learn, to enjoy, and to get inspired. I still do!

A Museum Adventure is full of artworks, artifacts, and even a fossil. You can see the pieces that inspired me in real museums, made by artists from all around the world and from all periods of history. It was quite a learning experience for me to include different types of artwork in my book. I learned a lot about color and brushstrokes by studying images very closely. I am so accustomed to painting in my own way that it was fun to try using other artists' styles! Do you recognize any of the artists and paintings included in the book? Check out www.librarymousebooks.com for more information about the art in this book.

The illustrations in this book were made with Winsor and Newton gouache on Arches watercolor paper.

Cataloging-in-Publication Data has been applied for and may be obtained from the Library of Congress. ISBN 978-1-4197-0173-3

Book design by Chad W. Beckerman

Printed and bound in China
10 9 8 7 6 5 4 3 2 1

Abrams Books for Young Readers are available at special discounts when purchased in quantity for premiums and promotions as well as fundraising or educational use. Special editions can also be created to specification. For details, contact specialsales@abramsbooks.com or the address below.

ABRAMS
THE ART OF BOOKS SINCE 1949
115 West 18th Street
New York, NY 10011
www.abramsbooks.com